Smart Call

by PJ Gray

ISBN-13: 978-1-68021-112-2
ISBN-10: 1-68021-112-9
eBook: 978-1-63078-429-4

Printed in Guangzhou, China
NOR/1115/CA21501590

20 19 18 17 16   1 2 3 4 5

Jen stood at the store.
Her mom was late.

"Where is she?"

3

Jen stood there.
She was done with work.
She held a big bag.
Her **dress** was in it.

Jen saw a car.
It was her mom.
Jen got in.

"You are late.
Aunt Pam will be mad.
We will miss the
wedding."

Her mom shook her head.
"I am not late."

"It's an hour drive!"

"Yes," her mom said. "I
know. We will not miss it.
And I am not late. I wrote
down the **time**."

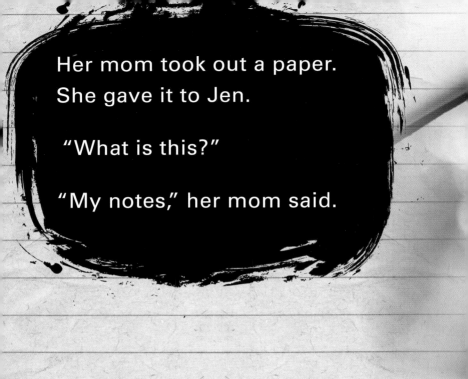

Her mom took out a paper.
She gave it to Jen.

"What is this?"

"My notes," her mom said.

"Paper notes?
Don't you use your phone?"

Jen's mom shook her head.
Her phone was old.
It was a flip phone.

"Mom, get a **smartphone**."

Jen held her smartphone. "I use my phone **calendar.** It keeps me on track."

"My phone has that," her mom said.

"Why don't you use it?"

"The **screen.** It is too small."

Jen shook her head.

Her mom drove on.
Time went by.
Jen's mom spoke.
"Check my purse."

"For what?"

"I made a list. It's on paper."

"A list? What for?"

"Stuff for the wedding."

Jen dug in the purse.
"I don't see it."

19

Jen held her phone up.
"My phone is **smart.**
I keep lists in it."

Her mom shook her head.
"I don't need that."

Day of Wedding:

-paint nails

-pick up dress

-meet mom at 3:30

Her mom drove on.
Time went by.
Jen's mom was upset.
"I need that list.
It has a name on it."

"A name," said Jen.
"What name?"

"The **flower shop.**
Your aunt needs our help.
We have to pick up flowers."

"Where is the shop?"

"Stone Street."

Jen got out her phone.
"Jane's Flower Shop?"

"Yes. That's it! How did you find it?"

"My phone. It can search
the **web.**"

"Can my phone do that?"

"No," Jen said.

WEB🔍
SEARCH

🔍 flower shop

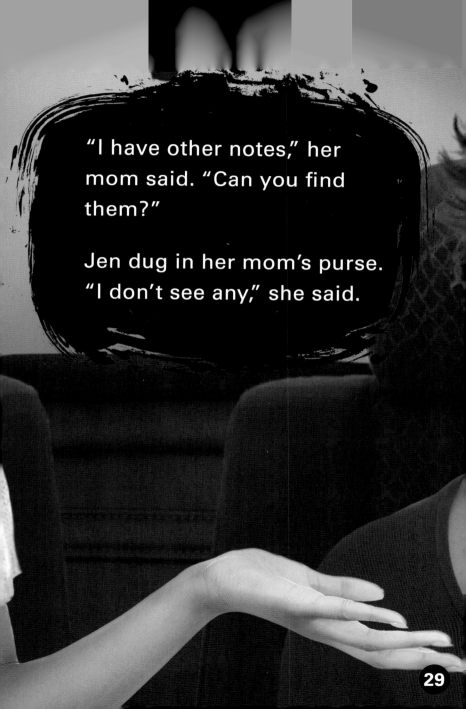

"I have other notes," her mom said. "Can you find them?"

Jen dug in her mom's purse. "I don't see any," she said.

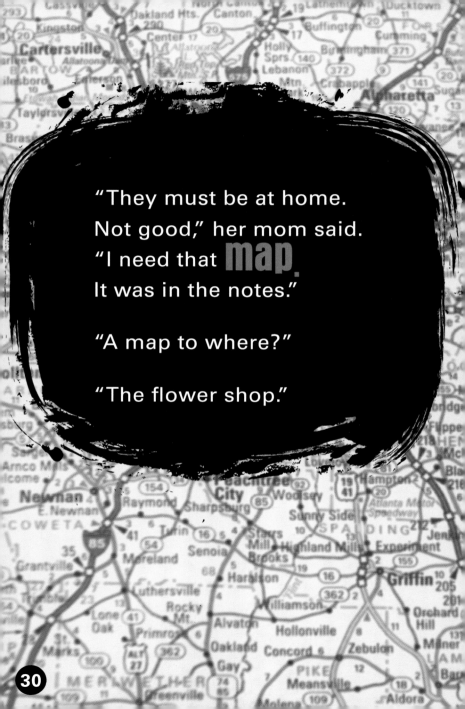

"They must be at home.
Not good," her mom said.
"I need that map.
It was in the notes."

"A map to where?"

"The flower shop."

- Left at Main
- Right on Oak
- Right on Stone

31

Jen had her smartphone.
She put in the **address.**
"I got it!"

"How? Wait! Don't tell me.
Your phone has maps."

"Yep."

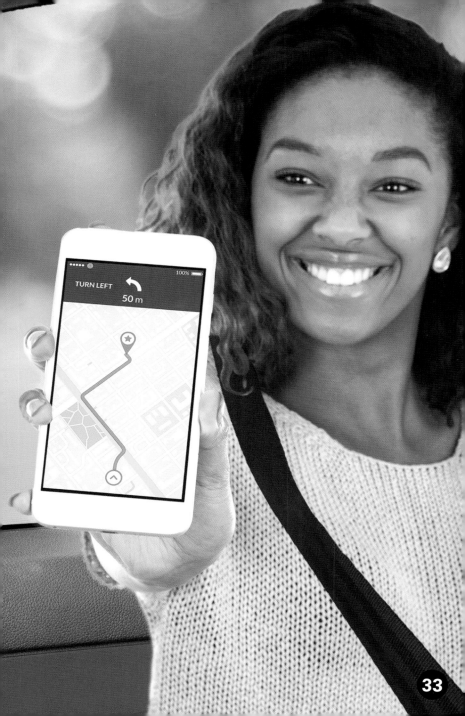

TURN LEFT
50 m
100%

"Here," her mom said.
"Take my phone. It can
still do things."

"Like what?"

"Make phone calls!
Call your aunt. Tell her
we are okay."

Jen did. But the call did not go through. **"No signal."**

"Are you sure?"

Jen took out her phone. She got a strong signal.

Jen made the call.
Her aunt did not pick up.
So Jen sent her a text.

The wedding was very soon.
They got the **flowers.**
And drove on.

"Find the church," Jen's mom said. "Hurry! Use your phone."

"Use my phone? Not yours?"

"Don't joke. We have to hurry."

"Found it!" Jen said. "It's close."

TURN RIGHT

100%

They got to the church.
Jen's aunt was there.
"You made it," she said. "And you are **on time!** Now hurry. You still need to change."

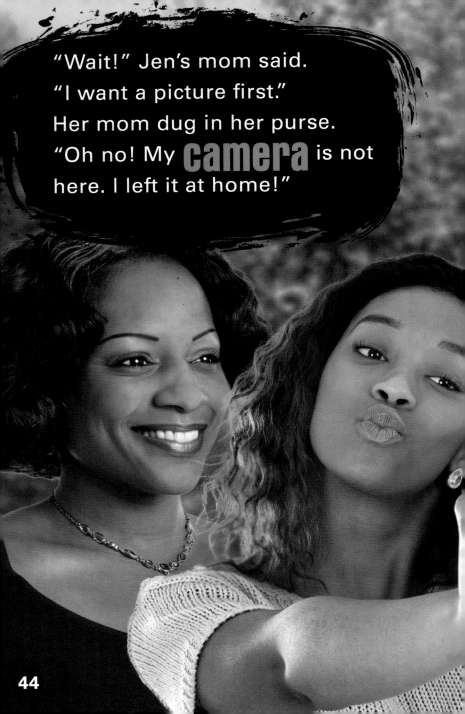

"Wait!" Jen's mom said. "I want a picture first." Her mom dug in her purse. "Oh no! My **camera** is not here. I left it at home!"

Jen took out her phone.
"Don't worry, Mom. Use this."

Jen's mom shook her head.
"I think it's time," she said.

"Time for what?"

"Time to get a
new phone."

phone home

PHONE SHOP

SALE!

TEEN EMERGENT READER LIBRARIES®

BOOSTERS

The Literacy Revolution Continues with New TERL Booster Titles!

Each Sold Individually

9781680211542

9781680211139

9781680211528

9781680211153

9781680211122

ENGAGE [2]

9781680211146

9781680211337

9781680211290

9781680211535

9781680211313

EXCEL [3]

9781680211306

9781680211320

NEW TITLES COMING SOON!
www.jointheliteracyrevolution.com